WILD PONIES ON THE MOOR!

May heard a pattering like the sound of rain. She looked left and saw the ponies running toward them. The lead one had his head up, mane flashing. His small hooves picked their way neatly through the heather. On the pony's nose was a leather stripe.

"Is he wearing a halter?" May asked her father.

"Looks that way," Mr. Grover said. "Sometimes wild ponies are captured and trained. Most of them don't mind. But some of them can't stand it and they break free."

"He was trained once?" May said.

"Maybe, and he didn't like it, so he took off," said Mr. Grover.

May Goes
to England

BONNIE BRYANT

Illustrated by Marcy Ramsey

A SKYLARK BOOK
NEW YORK • TORONTO • LONDON • SYDNEY • AUCKLAND

RL 3, 007–010
MAY GOES TO ENGLAND
A Bantam Skylark Book / May 1997

ISBN 0-553-48481-8

*Bantam Books are published by Bantam Books, a division of Bantam
Doubleday Dell Publishing Group, Inc. Its trademark, consisting of the
words "Bantam Books" and the portrayal of a rooster, is Registered in
U.S. Patent and Trademark Office and in other countries. Marca
Registrada. Bantam Books, 1540 Broadway, New York, New York
10036.*

PRINTED IN THE UNITED STATES OF AMERICA

OPM   0   9   8   7   6   5   4   3   2   1

*I would like to give my special thanks
to Helen Geraghty for her help
in the writing of this book.*

Hi, we're the **PONY TAILS**—May Grover, Corey Takamura, and Jasmine James. We're neighbors, we're best friends, and most of all, we're pony-crazy.

My name is **May.** My pony is named Macaroni after my favorite food, macaroni and cheese. He's the sweetest pony in the world! He never loses his temper. Jasmine and Corey say he's the exact opposite of me. Of course, they're just teasing. I have two older sisters who say I'm a one-girl disaster area, but they're not teasing. Would you like some used sisters? I have two for sale.

I'm called **Corey**—short for Corinne. I live between Jasmine and May—in a lot of ways. My house is between theirs. I'm between them in personality, too. Jasmine's organized, May's forgetful, and I can be both. May's impulsive, Jasmine's cautious, and I'm just reasonable. My pony is named Samurai. He's got a white blaze on his face shaped like a samurai sword. Sam is temperamental, but he's mine and I love him.

I'm **Jasmine.** My pony is named Outlaw. His face is white, like an outlaw's mask. He can be as unpredictable as an outlaw, too, but I'd never let him go to jail because I love him to pieces! I like to ride him, and I also like to look after him. I have a baby sister named Sophie. When she gets older I'm going to teach her to ride.

So why don't you tack up and have fun with us on our pony adventures!

May Corey Jasmine

JASMINE'S HOUSE

COREY'S HOUSE

MAY'S HOUSE

May Goes
to England

1 A Poem About Piskies

"I don't want to hear another word about piskies," May said grumpily.

"But they sound so cool," Jasmine said.

"Piskies are not cool," May said. "They're pesky."

May's family, the Grovers, were about to go to Cornwall, England. According to May's older sisters, Dottie and Ellie, Cornwall was loaded with piskies, who hated little girls.

" 'Piskies are invisible people,' " Jasmine read from the guidebook that Dottie and Ellie had given May. " 'They sit on mushrooms, which are called pisky stools. They love to tease people.' " Jasmine looked up with a grin. "Especially people who are messy."

"What a surprise!" May said. For weeks Dottie and Ellie had been telling her that the piskies of Cornwall were going to make her life miserable.

"There's a poem about piskies," Jasmine said.

> "See-saw, Margery Daw,
>   Sold her bed and lay on the straw,
>   Sold her bed and lay upon hay,
>   Pisky came and took her away."

May looked around her room. It was messier than usual because she was packing for the trip. But then, it was always kind of messy. May didn't really believe that there were such things as piskies who took messy people away. On the other hand, when she got to Cornwall, maybe she should be extra neat, just in case.

"There are giants, too," Jasmine said, looking at the book. "They eat people who get lost on the moor."

"What's a moor?" Corey said.

2

Jasmine looked in the book. "A wet, soggy wasteland with no houses or trees. Travelers often get lost there."

"Cornwall sounds like an ideal vacation spot," said Corey with a laugh.

"Hey, the moor is full of ponies," May said. "The ponies have been living there hundreds of years. By the next time you see me, I'll be a wild pony expert." May was trying to look on the bright side of things. When she'd first heard that her family would be exchanging houses with a farm family in Cornwall, she had been excited. But since Dottie and Ellie had started telling her about piskies, she had her doubts.

"It says here that the moor is filled with huge stone toothpicks," said Jasmine, looking at the guidebook. "Giants use them to clean their teeth."

"Yeah, a giant wouldn't want a human to get stuck in his teeth," Corey said.

"Can we talk about something else?" May said.

"Totally," Jasmine said. "We'll talk about pirates." She turned a page. "It says here that pirates used to build fake

3

lighthouses. Ships would steer toward them and crash on the rocks and the pirates would rob them."

"My father says that Cornwall is completely safe," May said. "He says that there aren't any more pirates in Cornwall and that giants and piskies are imaginary."

"Then you'll have a great time," said Jasmine, shutting the book. "Just don't go wandering around the moor when the moon is full. That's when the giants and piskies come out."

"Gee, thanks," May said.

Mrs. Grover stuck her head into May's room. "Are you done packing?" she asked May. "We'll be loading the car soon."

"I'm done," May said.

As soon as Mrs. Grover left, Corey and Jasmine looked in May's suitcase.

"Aren't you forgetting something?" Jasmine asked.

May checked her suitcase. In addition to her regular clothes, she had a pair of riding boots, two pairs of breeches, and

her riding helmet. "What else is there?" she asked.

"A hairbrush?" Jasmine said.

"Details," May muttered. She went into the bathroom to get her hairbrush. Then she saw her toothbrush. That would be handy, too, she realized. And then there was toothpaste. Two weeks without toothpaste would be awful. She reached under the sink and found a plastic traveling bag and packed all her toiletries inside.

She came back into her bedroom and plunked the bag into the corner of her suitcase. "That's it." She closed the suitcase and zipped it. Suddenly she realized that she was really, truly leaving home.

"I'm going to miss you guys," she said.

Corey hugged her. "You'll write."

"Right," May said. "I'll definitely write." She sighed. "If only I were going on this trip with you guys, and not my evil sisters."

"You'll survive," Jasmine said.

"Ha," said May.

The three of them hugged. It was a big Pony Tail hug. The Pony Tails weren't a club; they were best friends and next-door neighbors. It was hard for May to imagine two weeks away from Corey and Jasmine. It would be even harder to be away from her pony.

"What about Macaroni?" said May. Macaroni was her pony.

"He'll be fine," Jasmine said. "We'll visit him every day. Twice a day."

"Three times a day," Corey said.

"He'll get plenty of exercise. The farmer's son will ride him," Jasmine said.

"I'm really glad the family from Cornwall will be staying in our house while we stay in theirs," May said. "And I'm really glad they have a son who wants to ride Macaroni. But there's something creepy I didn't tell you."

Jasmine's and Corey's eyes widened. "What?" said Corey.

"His name," May said. "You know what it is?"

Corey and Jasmine shook their heads.

"Wilfred," said May. "Isn't that weird?"

2 A Pony Named Cheddar

"Merry Meeting! What kind of name is that?" said Ellie, reading the name of the tiny town in Cornwall they were driving into. It was the Grover family's third day in England, and they were exploring the countryside.

"Merry Meeting, ha!" Dottie said. "Miserable Meeting is more like it."

"Where do they get these stupid names?" said Ellie. "Cheesewring. Washaway. The Devil's Frying Pan. What's their problem?"

"Cornwall has been around for a long time," Mr. Grover said. "Those names are hundreds of years old."

"How come I'm not surprised?" Ellie said glumly. "This place is as much fun as a museum."

After tormenting May about how much she would hate Cornwall, Dottie and Ellie were the ones who hated it. To their horror, they had discovered that Cornwall had no shopping mall. It didn't have a radio station that played rock and roll. Dottie and Ellie were in despair.

"Too bad the farmhouse doesn't have TV," said May. "But that's okay. You can listen to old Cornish songs on the radio."

Ellie slumped in the backseat. "This is going to be the longest two weeks of my life."

"Cheer up," May said. "I hear there's folk dancing on the village green."

Dottie looked as if she was about to faint.

May, on the other hand, was having a great time. She had been a little nervous about coming to Cornwall, but now she liked it. The farmhouse was a big old rambling stone building with something called a cheese safe. At first May thought it was to keep cheese from being stolen.

But then she found out that it was a place to keep cheese cool. The house also had a chicken coop, where May gathered fresh eggs for breakfast. For dinner they had meat pies called pasties. Mrs. Grover said they were pronounced *pass-tees*. They were golden brown and delicious. Best of all, the farm had ponies and horses.

There were three ponies, and her father had told her that she could ride any one she wanted. Her favorite was Cheddar, the pony who belonged to the farmer's son. Cheddar was named after cheddar cheese, which is very popular in England. The pony wasn't the color of cheese. He was actually a dark bay. But he had the personality of cheddar cheese—he was bold and sharp. That made him a nice contrast to her own pony, Macaroni, who was mellow and sweet. In her first letter to Corey and Jasmine, May said that at last she had found the ideal combination of ponies: Cheddar and Macaroni—in other words, macaroni and cheese.

"What do they do for fun here?" asked Ellie. "Or maybe they don't have fun."

Mr. Grover said, "They go for walks on the moor. They ride."

"Fabulous," Ellie groaned.

"I know a place you'd like," May said. "The Bodmin Gaol Museum." When Ellie didn't answer, May explained, "*Gaol* is English for *jail*. It's spelled *g-a-o-l*, but you pronounce it *j-a-i-l*. They have a real, true dungeon in the museum." She said to Mr. Grover, "Why don't we drop Dottie and Ellie off there?"

Mr. Grover didn't say anything, but May saw that he was grinning. Ever since the Grovers had arrived in Cornwall, Dottie and Ellie had been driving everyone crazy.

"They could put them in leg irons," said May helpfully.

"That's enough, May," said Mr. Grover.

"I bet the piskies have seen the hideous mess May made of her room," Dottie said.

May thought of her room at the farmhouse. It wasn't really messy. It was just . . . *cluttered*. She had meant to clean it up, but she had been too busy. She decided that as soon as she got back to the farm she'd turn it into the neatest room on earth.

"Piskies love to torture little girls," Ellie said.

"Who's little?" May muttered.

"They're waiting until midnight of the first full moon, and then they're going to get you," Dottie said.

"Personally, at midnight I'm planning to be asleep," May said.

"Just wait," said Ellie.

"Girls!" Mrs. Grover said. She sounded annoyed.

Mr. Grover steered over the top of the hill. It still amazed May that he had to drive on the left. He drove past a lorry (a truck) on the right and into the courtyard of the farmhouse.

The Grovers got out and stretched. Mr. Grover turned to May and said, "After sitting all day, I wouldn't mind a ride."

"Great idea," May said. At home her father was usually busy training horses.

But here he had plenty of time to ride with her.

May raced into the house and up the stairs to change. She loved her room here. It had a slanting ceiling, a huge wooden trunk that looked like a pirate chest, and a chair that was shaped like a triangle. Most important, it had lots of pony posters. Wilfred, the boy who lived here, might have a creepy name, but he certainly loved ponies. May's favorite poster was of a dark bay pony running across the moor, his mane and tail blowing back in the wind.

May dumped her clothes on the floor and looked around for her riding gear. Her breeches were next to the wastebasket, her shirt was on the window seat, and her riding hat was on top of the chest. But where were her riding boots? She distinctly remembered stepping out of them and leaving them in the middle of the floor.

She was about to go downstairs and ask her mother if she'd seen the boots, when she noticed the closet door.

Fat chance that she might have put her

boots in the closet. She decided to look anyway.

The boots were inside, standing neatly next to each other.

Never in her life had May left her boots standing neatly next to each other.

What did this mean? For a second May had the creeps. Her mother wouldn't have put the boots in the closet because she insisted that May had to put away her own clothes. Could it have been Dottie and Ellie? This seemed to be too clever a prank for them.

Could it have been piskies? According to Dottie and Ellie, this was just the kind of thing that piskies did. They loved to make people nervous.

But piskies aren't real, May told herself.

"May," came Mr. Grover's voice from outside.

"Coming," May called out the window. She pulled on the boots and ran downstairs.

Her father was already sitting on Spock, the farmer's big bay horse.

"Is something wrong?" he said. "You have a funny look on your face."

"No way," May said. "Everything is great." She ran into the barn.

Cheddar was in his stall, switching his tail from side to side as if he couldn't figure out why she was being so slow.

"Somebody moved my boots," May told him.

Cheddar yawned. He wasn't interested. He wanted to go riding.

"Okay, okay," May said.

She got Cheddar's bridle and saddle and tacked him up as fast as she could. Then she led him out to the courtyard.

"That was fast," Mr. Grover said.

"Cheddar is ready to go," she said. "I am, too."

"I was thinking we could ride up to the moor," Mr. Grover said. "We haven't been there yet."

May remembered that the moor was where piskies lured messy people to be eaten by giants. "Or we could ride up the creek to the waterfall," she said.

"We did that yesterday," Mr. Grover said.

"We could go to the sheep farm," May said.

15

"Sure," said Mr. Grover, but he looked disappointed.

May realized that she was being silly. Bodmin Moor was one of the big sights of Cornwall. She had to go there. She would be safe with her father.

"Let's go to the moor," she said.

As they crossed the stone bridge, Cheddar's and Spock's hooves echoed against the pavement. On the far side there was a clump of purple weeds. Cheddar tried to grab a bite, but May tightened the reins.

They began to climb. Cheddar walked swiftly up the hill. May felt the air getting colder. Cheddar trotted the last few yards to the top.

May stopped next to her father. Ahead of them was the moor. It looked like a huge green blanket, May thought, fuzzy and almost featureless. A hawk circled overhead.

"There's some moor mist," Mr. Grover said. He pointed to a far corner of the moor where a finger of fog seemed to rise directly out of the ground.

"It's beautiful," Mr. Grover said softly.

May looked at him. *Beautiful* was not the word that sprang into her mind. *Creepy* was more like it.

"Look there," Mr. Grover said.

He was pointing at the mist. May had never known her father was so into mist. But there was something coming out of the mist. May's stomach lurched.

"It's the most amazing sight on earth," Mr. Grover said.

May saw legs racing out of the mist, and a mane, and a flying tail. It was a dark bay pony like the one on the poster in her room. The pony was followed by a stream of ponies racing across the moor. They made May think of racehorses, except that they weren't racing anywhere. There was no finish line, no prize. They were racing for the joy of it.

"Wow," May said. Reading about wild ponies was one thing; seeing them was another. She imagined what it would be like to ride a wild pony. Then she realized that that was what made them wild—nobody rode them.

Suddenly the moor didn't seem so terrible. "So what are we waiting for?" asked May. "Let's go."

Mr. Grover grinned. "I knew you'd like it." He must have given Spock a signal because Spock raised his head, shook his bridle, and picked his way neatly onto the narrow trail.

May looked down. The heather was tangled. She knew there were hidden streams underfoot, but she didn't care. She wanted to ride on this moor. She pressed her legs against Cheddar's sides and he took off with an easy, high-stepping trot. The pink heather flowers flew past. May could smell something heavy and sweet, like honey.

Ahead, her father turned with a thumbs-up gesture to ask if she wanted to canter. She nodded enthusiastically.

Spock broke into a canter. Cheddar followed with an easy, rocking gait. The heather was a blur. They cantered and cantered until May felt like a wild pony herself, running free in the sunlight.

Mr. Grover stopped to wait for her beside a tall, skinny rock that poked out of the heather. "This is a monolith," he said. "Monoliths are one of the most famous features of the moor. Hundreds and hundreds of years ago, people left them here. But no one knows exactly why."

May gave the monolith a cautious look. "Er . . . could that be a giant's toothpick?"

Mr. Grover laughed. "That's what they call them."

May made a note to mention the giant's toothpick in her next letter to Jasmine and Corey.

May heard a pattering like the sound of rain. She looked left and saw the ponies running toward them. The lead one had his head up, mane flashing. His small hooves picked their way neatly through the tangled heather. On the pony's nose was a leather stripe.

"Is he wearing a halter?" May asked her father.

"Looks that way," Mr. Grover said. "Sometimes wild ponies are captured and trained. Most of them don't mind.

But some of them can't stand it and they break free."

"He was trained once?" May said.

"Maybe, and he didn't like it, so he took off," said Mr. Grover.

3 Corey and Jasmine Meet Wilfred

"Here goes," Corey said. She raised her hand to knock on the Grovers' back door, but then she didn't knock because she was worried about Wilfred. What kind of kid would have a name like that?

It had been four days since May left, and every day Corey and Jasmine had resolved to go meet Wilfred. But then each day they had put it off.

"We promised May we'd check him out," Jasmine said. "She'll be furious if we don't."

Corey knew that Jasmine was right. She knocked.

A woman in a flowered dress answered the door.

"Is . . . er . . . Wilfred here?" said Jasmine.

"Indeed he is. You must be the neighbor girls," said the woman, except when she said *girls* it sounded more like *gells*.

"That's us," said Corey cheerfully. Later, she knew, she and Jasmine could have a giggle over being called *gells*.

"I'll fetch him directly," the woman said. "By the way, I'm Mrs. Neill."

It sounded so formal that Corey wondered if she should curtsy or something.

"I'm Corey," Corey said.

"I'm Jasmine."

"Indeed you are," Mrs. Neill said. She smiled in a rather stiff way and left.

Corey and Jasmine exchanged looks.

"May is going to owe us big-time," muttered Corey.

A minute later Mrs. Neill came back with a boy who had long brown hair and a high forehead. He had solemn brown eyes and a serious mouth. He was wearing blue jeans and a T-shirt, but Corey

figured that he was probably trying to go native, wearing what dumb Americans wore.

"I live next door," Corey said. "I'm Corey."

"She has a totally insane dog," Jasmine said. "Maybe you heard him howling. If you think he's bad, you should meet her parrot. He's even worse. And then there's her goat, Alexander, otherwise known as Alexander the Goat." The girls giggled.

"Rather," Wilfred said without smiling.

Corey and Jasmine exchanged looks. Wilfred was not going to be a barrel of laughs. But a promise was a promise.

"Do you want to come with us to visit Macaroni?" Corey asked.

"The little yellow pony?" Wilfred said. "Indeed, I've been riding him."

Corey was steamed. Macaroni was not a little yellow pony. He was the greatest, the gentlest, the smartest, the funniest. He was *not* some ordinary little yellow pony.

"I guess you could say that," Corey said crossly.

The three of them walked out to the barn in silence.

"I suppose you have a zillion ponies at home," Jasmine said. "Living on the edge of the moor the way you do."

"Not a zillion," Wilfred said. "That would be rather much."

Behind his back, Corey and Jasmine exchanged looks.

They took Wilfred into Macaroni's stall. Macaroni nuzzled them and looked at them with worried brown eyes, wondering where May was.

"Hi, Macaroni," Corey said. "I know you miss May, but I'm sure you're enjoying taking Wilfred for rides." But then Corey wondered if she was lying to the pony.

"Actually, we have been enjoying one another," Wilfred said. He tickled Macaroni on his forehead, under his forelock.

"Mac could probably use a ride right now," Corey said.

"So we'll saddle up then, shall we?" Wilfred said.

The girls raced off to get their own ponies, and fifteen minutes later they were all riding around the ring. It was obvious that Wilfred knew a lot about riding. His seat was firm. His heels were down. He held the reins with a light but firm touch. Macaroni looked content.

Corey realized that she and Jasmine could learn a few things from Wilfred, but on the other hand, who wanted to? She had the distinct feeling that Wilfred was showing off.

"Would you care to trot?" Corey said.

"Rather," Wilfred said.

As they trotted, Wilfred posted easily. And when they cantered, Corey thought Wilfred looked positively bored. This wasn't like riding with May. There was no friendship, no fun, no jokes.

After a while Corey said to Wilfred, "Well, I guess we'll take off. We've got lots to do." She looked at Jasmine.

"Actually," Jasmine said with a grin, "what we have to do is go to my house and have homemade cookies and apple juice. Want to come along?"

Corey made a face. She'd had enough of Wilfred for one day.

"Rather," Wilfred said.

As Corey and Jasmine rode off, Corey said, "Why did you have to do that?"

"He's a guest," Jasmine said. "He's a stranger here."

"Strange is right," Corey grumbled.

Half an hour later Corey and Jasmine were sitting at the round table in the Jameses' kitchen. Jasmine had set out three glasses of apple juice and a plate of her mother's homemade peanut butter cookies.

"This is going to be a laugh and a half," Corey said.

"Will you lighten up?" Jasmine said.

There was a knock at the door. Jasmine went to open it. Wilfred was standing there, holding a baking pan filled with custard, cake, and fruit.

"Come in," Jasmine said. She led Wilfred through the mudroom into the kitchen.

"This is for you," he said shyly, holding out the baking pan. "My mother made it. It's a trifle."

"It's not a trifle at all," Jasmine said, gazing down at the yellow, delicious-looking concoction. "It looks like a big deal to me."

"Er," Wilfred said, "trifle is a name for an English treat."

Jasmine put the pan on the table. She got three plates and three spoons. She passed them out, and then the three of them sat there looking at the trifle. "You first," she said to Wilfred.

"No, you," he said.

We could spend the rest of our lives waiting for someone to go first, Corey thought.

With a grin Jasmine pulled the trifle pan closer and gave herself a large serving. "Somehow I think I'm going to enjoy this," she said. She looked at Wilfred and Corey, and since the two of them were just sitting there staring, she took a bite.

Jasmine's eyes opened wide. "This is good." She took another bite. "It's not good, it's outstanding." Jasmine looked at the pan of trifle as if she was figuring out how large a second helping she could take.

Corey's stomach growled. She was always hungry after riding. And now she was truly hungry. She had been planning to ignore the trifle, but now she realized that if she waited too long, it would be gone. She pulled the pan toward her and scooped out a small helping. She took a bite. It was creamy with chunks of fruit. It was so-so, she thought. But maybe she should give it another chance. She took another bite. It was not half bad.

Next thing Corey knew, she had emptied her bowl. She looked up and saw that Wilfred had served himself and that Jasmine had taken a second helping, but there was still plenty left for her. She gave herself a large serving because, after all, her last serving had been pretty small. She started eating quickly, but then she slowed down because she wanted to make this trifle last.

"I really like it," Corey said. And then she couldn't help herself and she said, "Rather!"

Wilfred burst out laughing.

Corey took a second look. Perhaps Wilfred was human after all.

"You know what?" she said. "I think Mac likes you."

"Mac is great," Wilfred said.

Corey realized that maybe she'd been mean to Wilfred. She remembered when she had been new in Willow Creek. She remembered how shy she'd felt. She remembered how worried she'd been that Jasmine and May wouldn't like her.

She ran her spoon around the bowl, hunting for a last crumb of trifle. She found one and licked her spoon. "Can I ask you something?"

"Ask away," Wilfred said.

"Where'd you get your name?" Corey asked.

"Corey!" Jasmine said.

"I don't mind," Wilfred said. "Wilfred *is* kind of wet."

"Wet?" Corey said.

"Er . . . dorky," Wilfred said. "Isn't that what you Americans say?"

Corey and Jasmine burst out laughing. "Sometimes," Jasmine said.

"But what I can do? I'm a Wilfred," he said.

Corey was struck with a sudden burst of inspiration. "When you're in America you're not a Wilfred, you're a Will."

"I'm into it," he said with a grin.

"Will," Jasmine said, "have one of my mother's cookies. They're almost as good as your mother's trifle."

Will took a cookie and bit into it. "Better, I should think," he said.

The three of them munched happily on the cookies.

"What's your house like?" Corey asked.

"A terrible old dump, really," Will said.

"That means you like it," Corey said with a grin. "You see, I'm learning to understand English English."

"It's in a valley," Will said, "but if you ride up the hill you're on the moor. A moor is . . ."

"Treeless and boggy," said Jasmine, remembering the guidebook. "A place where travelers get lost."

Will looked serious. "A moor is the best place for riding—ever."

4 Four Kinds of Jam

"We're going to have a nonriding day today," Mrs. Grover said. "I promised your sisters. If we don't, they'll become unbearable."

"Gee, I thought they were unbearable already," May said.

Mr. Grover walked into the kitchen. He was wearing pants and a sport shirt instead of his usual riding breeches and hacking jacket. He looked handsome.

Something appeared in the doorway. It was black, orange, and leopardy. It was Dottie wearing a black miniskirt, orange shoes, and a fake leopard top.

"Dottie, you can't wear that," said Mrs.

Grover in horror. "We're going to a tea shop."

Dottie put her hands on her hips. "I suppose you want me to wear some kind of stupid flowered dress."

"Flowered dresses are very nice," said Mrs. Grover.

"That's it!" Dottie threw herself into a chair. "It's not like this vacation wasn't a nightmare to begin with."

But no one was looking at her because Ellie had entered. She was wearing a purple satin dress with a huge gold belt, earrings that went down to her shoulders, and bright green shoes.

"Oh," Mrs. Grover said. "You know, dear, I don't think that's exactly right."

"This is the first time I look decent all vacation and you want me to change," Ellie said bitterly.

"Ahhh-hem," came a sound from the other side of the room. Everyone turned.

Mr. Grover was usually cheerful and easygoing, but it was clear that he was steamed. "It's time to get started," he said.

"Come on, you two fashion statements," May said to her sisters. "Let's go."

The family piled into the car.

"We're going to the Lizard. That's a famous peninsula with cliffs and moors," Mr. Grover said.

"Be still, my heart," Dottie muttered.

"But first, we have to pass through Gweek," Mr. Grover said.

"Hey, they named a town after you guys," May said to Dottie and Ellie.

As they drove through Goonhilly Downs, which was a moor, Mr. Grover explained that there used to be wild ponies there. He said that they'd been dark bay, like the Bodmin Moor ponies.

"Fascinating," Ellie muttered.

May looked out the window at the fuzzy green hills, trying to imagine ponies. Too bad they were gone.

The car reached the top of a hill. Below, May could see the ocean. It was blue-green and endless. It's kind of like the moor, she thought. It would be easy to lose your way.

The cliffs were dotted with tiny bright flowers. May opened the window, and in floated a wonderful smell, a combination of flowers and sea and sunlight.

"You're ruining my hair," Dottie said.

"That would be impossible," May said as she sat back.

Mr. Grover drove the car into a parking lot on the top of the cliffs. "Who wants to walk down to the sea?" he said.

"I do," said May.

"I do," said Mrs. Grover.

Dottie and Ellie didn't say a thing.

Mrs. Grover said, "You two are not going to spend the whole vacation inside the car. You are joining us."

Dottie and Ellie groaned and dragged themselves out of the car.

The trail zigzagged past the tea shop, which was halfway down the cliff. May, who was wearing sneakers, didn't have any trouble. But Dottie and Ellie slipped and slid and bumped into bushes. By the time they got to the bottom, they were covered with dust.

"That look is you," May said.

Ellie's eyes filled with tears.

"What's wrong?" Mrs. Grover asked, looking worried.

"I broke a fingernail," Ellie said.

Mrs. Grover sighed. "You'll feel better after a nice cup of tea."

They walked back up to the tea shop by an easier route.

"This is England's southernmost tea shop," Mrs. Grover said.

"Tea," Dottie said. "Gross."

"And scones, and jam, and cream," Mrs. Grover said.

Dottie and Ellie looked slightly more cheerful.

When they got to the tea shop, every woman and girl there was wearing casual clothes. Dottie and Ellie looked strange, to say the least. But no one stared at them. In England, May realized, people don't stare.

Dottie and Ellie looked uncomfortable. "Who needs scones?" said Dottie to Ellie. "Let's go for a walk." They took off.

May loved teatime. There were scones, still hot from the oven, thick clotted cream, a bowl of fresh strawberries, and four kinds of jam. Since May was planning to write to Corey and Jasmine to tell them about life in England, she felt that it was her responsibility to try all four kinds of jam. All four were delicious, but she liked the gooseberry jam the best. It was greenish—not a great color for jam, May thought—but it was tangy and sweet.

As Mr. and Mrs. Grover and May sat back after finishing their tea, May said, "Cornwall is great."

"I knew you would like it," Mr. Grover said.

"Wild ponies, four kinds of jam—what could be better?" May said.

When they got to the parking lot at the top of the cliff, Dottie and Ellie were sitting on a bench, deep in conversation. Dottie was holding a bag.

"So what were you girls up to?" Mrs. Grover said.

"Nothing much," Dottie said.

"What did you buy?" Mrs. Grover asked.

"Dumb Cornwall stuff," Ellie said. "You have to buy something. I mean, if you don't buy something, all your friends will laugh."

They got back in the car.

"Let's take the coast road home," Mr. Grover said.

"Good idea," said Mrs. Grover.

The road wound along the edge of the cliff. From below, May could hear the crashing of the waves. Suddenly the car stopped.

"What's up?" May said.

"It's one-way traffic here," Mr. Grover said. "We have to wait for the cars from the other direction to come through."

May looked ahead and saw that the road was very narrow.

"How come they don't make the road wider?" May asked.

"If they make the road wider, piskies tear it down," Dottie said.

"Gee, how come I didn't know that?" May said.

"You know why the cliffs are so steep?" Ellie said. "Giants split the rocks with their bare hands."

"You guys should get other interests," May said.

The road ahead was clear, and it was

time for the Grovers' car to pass through. Mr. Grover steered along the narrow road.

May closed her eyes. She could ride a pony all day long without getting tired, but a car journey was something else. She felt pooped.

A while later she felt the car turn and stop. She opened her eyes and saw that they were back at the farmhouse. It was beginning to get dark.

"That was a wonderful drive," Mrs. Grover said.

May climbed out of the car and stretched. They had been away from the farm all day. She realized that Cheddar might be lonely. She went into the kitchen and grabbed an apple and went out to the barn.

When she walked into Cheddar's stall, he turned and looked at her as if he'd been wondering where she was all day.

"We went to the Lizard," May said. "And then we ate in England's southernmost tea shop."

Cheddar sighed.

May put the apple on her palm. Cheddar bit it and then chewed. He looked at her as if to say thank you, and then his eyelids dropped and his eyes closed. He was dozing. This was a sleepy kind of day, May thought.

When May got back to the farmhouse kitchen, Dottie and Ellie looked almost normal. They were wearing blue jeans and T-shirts and sneakers.

"Dottie and I are going for a walk," Ellie said.

"Good for you," Mrs. Grover said. "I'm glad you're finally beginning to enjoy this vacation. But don't stay too long. It's getting dark."

May yawned. She climbed the stairs to her room. In the doorway she stopped to look. True, her room was a bit messy. But right this minute she was sleepy. She'd pick up in the morning.

She took off her dress and dropped it on the window seat, and then she slipped into her pony T-shirt and her pony shorts. She walked over to the bed. It looked so soft, so welcoming. She dived under the covers and fell fast asleep.

In her dream May smelled heather. She

could feel a pony moving under her. She
looked down. He was a dark bay and he
was running with fast, easy steps. The
pony jumped a creek. Something tickled
her hands. It was the pony's mane blowing back in the wind. He was heading up-
ward toward the moon, which got larger,
and larger, and larger.

The moon exploded.

May sat up, her heart pounding, her
breath coming fast. This wasn't a dream.
It was real. A beam of blinding light filled
her room.

5 Alexander Is Missing!

"This is weird. Alexander is always here," Corey said.

Corey and Jasmine were saying good-night to Samurai, Corey's pony. Usually Alexander the Goat slept next to Samurai in his stall. But Alexander was nowhere to be seen. Samurai, otherwise known as Sam, looked lonely.

"We'll find him," Corey said. Sam might be as bold and brave as a Samurai warrior, but he was also sensitive. Corey could tell he missed the goat.

The door to the feed room was closed, and so was the door to the tack room.

"It's a mystery," Jasmine said.

They checked the field behind the Takamuras' barn and the yard next to the Takamuras' house. They checked the Jameses' yard and barn and didn't find him.

"Let's go ask Will if he's seen Alexander," Corey said.

They followed the Pony Trail, which was a path that led through the backyards of the three Pony Tails' houses. They knocked on the Grovers' back door.

Mrs. Neill appeared. "Hullo, Corey. Hullo, Jasmine," she said. Corey thought she seemed a lot more friendly now.

Will appeared behind her.

"Alexander the Goat is missing," Corey said. "We can't find him anywhere."

"Maybe we should ask Macaroni," Will said.

"Good idea," Corey said.

They walked into the Grovers' barn and there was Alexander, sound asleep in Macaroni's stall.

"Macaroni's stall door is fastened," Jasmine said. "How did he get in?"

"And my barn door was closed. How did he get out?" asked Corey.

"It must be magic," said Will with a smile.

6 Piskies Await

May blinked and rubbed her eyes.

From a shadow behind the beam of light came a whisper. "Piskies await. Come and meet your direful fate."

There was something familiar about this whisper.

"Piskies will try you in a green pisky ring," came the whisper.

"And you'll be guilty of everything," came another whisper.

May realized that it was Dottie and Ellie trying to scare the wits out of her.

May yawned and said, "Hey, I've always wanted to meet my doom." She swung her legs out of bed. "Lead me to it."

A small part of May's brain said that maybe it was better to stay in bed. But then she decided there was no way she was going to let Dottie and Ellie scare her. She put on her jeans and sneakers and her purple windbreaker and said, "Lead me to those pesky piskies."

As May walked into the hall, she looked toward her parents' room. She half expected to hear her father's sleepy voice asking what was going on. But no voice came.

They walked down the stairs. Dottie opened the front door.

"Green ring, pisky thing," Dottie said. "Soon May will be No-Thing."

"You guys have been watching too many cartoons," May said.

A full moon hung over the stable roof. The courtyard was filled with long, creepy shadows. May heard Cheddar snort behind the stable door. She would have given anything to put her arms around him and smell his warm pony smell right then. But Dottie and Ellie were walking toward the road that led up to the moor.

May trudged behind them to the top of the hill, feeling the damp night wind brushing against her skin. She looked back toward the farmhouse. No lights were on.

The moor looked as dark as waves in the ocean. Far off, May thought she saw a green ring.

"Scared?" Ellie asked.

"Totally terrified," May said casually.

"Piskies await. Can't be late," said Dottie.

May squinted, trying to see if there really was a green ring, but Dottie and Ellie were moving away. She had to follow them.

The trail was full of odd lumps and bumps. May knew they were just rocks, but she had to watch her feet to keep from tripping.

"This way," said Ellie, pointing into the dark, tangled heather.

Are we really going to walk through that stuff? May wondered. Even during the day it was hard to manage.

49

"Nervous?" Dottie said.

"Oh, totally," May said calmly.

She walked into the heather. It caught at her legs and ankles. It scratched her hands. May thought about her bed. She could have been asleep right that minute if Dottie and Ellie hadn't been such idiots.

She followed her sisters to a hilltop. Below them was a valley of dark heather.

They plunged down a trail. May wondered where Dottie and Ellie got the nerve to wander around the moor at night. Then she realized that they were so eager to tease her that they were temporarily brave.

They walked through a squishy bog. They fought their way through a patch of prickly gorse. May bumped against something and almost fell.

Over her shoulder Dottie said, "I told you to look out for those giant's toothpicks."

May looked at what she'd bumped into. It was one of those tall, skinny rocks that her father had pointed out to her—a monolith, a giant's toothpick. There are

50

no giants, she told herself. Absolutely no giants at all.

"Pisky doom, pisky gloom," Dottie whispered.

"Don't you wish you'd picked up your room?" Ellie whispered.

"That's just a stupid story," May said.

And then she saw it. An actual green ring. It couldn't be a pisky ring because there was no such thing as piskies.

"She's here. Piskies draw near," Dottie called out to the dark heather.

"Enter the ring, you guilty thing," said Ellie to May.

The heather rustled, looking like evil fingers reaching up from the ground. A cloud blew over the moon, throwing everything into darkness. The green ring was twice as bright now. May clutched her elbows. She wanted to run, but she wasn't going to run.

She was going to step right into that ring.

She half closed her eyes and moved forward.

No such thing as piskies, she whispered to herself. No such thing as piskies.

The ring was right ahead. She raised her foot. And stepped in.

Nothing happened. May looked down. There was something familiar about this ring. It looked like plastic.

May realized that the ring was made of the green glow-in-the-dark "fairy wands" sold in toy stores. Dottie and Ellie must have bought them while May and their parents were having tea. Then they must have come out earlier, while May was sleeping, to make the ring.

"Oh, piskies, yoo-hoo, I'm waiting," May said, crossing her arms. "I'm practically dying of terror."

Behind her, May heard Dottie mutter, "You and your big ideas. We didn't even scare her."

"It wasn't my big idea, it was your big idea," Ellie muttered back.

There was a sound behind May. She turned.

Coming over the top of the hill were wild ponies, their dark manes and tails glinting in the moonlight. Their heads were up, nostrils wide, eyes flashing.

"Run!" Dottie yelled.

"They won't hurt you," May said. But her voice was lost in the sounds of the ponies' hooves and her sisters' shrieks.

Ellie and Dottie ran wildly through the heather.

Then Ellie screamed—and disappeared.

7 Alone on the Moor!

May ran toward the spot where she had last seen Ellie.

Ellie was lying in a patch of flowers, her eyes closed, her breath coming fast.

May bent down. In the moonlight Ellie's lips looked blue. Her face was white. May touched Ellie's hand. Her skin felt clammy and cold. One of her feet was at a funny angle. For a second, May wanted to reach down and move Ellie's foot so that it wouldn't look so strange, but then she remembered that Max Regnery, the owner of Pine Hollow Stables, said that when someone had a fall they shouldn't

be moved because that could make things even worse.

Dottie came running up, her eyes wild. "What happened?" she said.

"Ellie twisted her ankle," May said, talking slowly and softly. She remembered how Max always stayed calm in an emergency.

Ellie whimpered. "It's broken," she said. "I can feel it." Tears ran out of the corners of her eyes and into her hair.

"We've got to do something," Dottie said. "Right now." Dottie looked around as if she expected to see a telephone.

"It's hopeless," Dottie said. "No one will ever find us. Ellie will go into shock. She'll die."

Ellie moaned.

May realized that this was something Ellie didn't need to hear. "Everything is going to be fine," she said to Ellie. "I'll go and get help."

"How?" Dottie said. "We're alone. We're helpless."

"Dottie!" May said.

Dottie stopped talking.

"Sit down next to her. Hold her hand," May said. "I'll be back soon."

Obediently Dottie sat down.

That was almost funny. Both Dottie and Ellie were doing exactly what May had told them to do. Did that make *her* an older sister? It made her *feel* like an older sister. She had to act like one, too. Ellie needed help, and May was the one who could get it for her.

"Don't move," she told her sisters. They weren't going anywhere.

May turned to the moor. It seemed vast and silent and empty, but she knew the answer was there, perhaps over the rise. Would piskies help a girl who needed to help a sister? She crossed her fingers and set out.

May climbed to the top of the hill and peered over. The sight beneath her took her breath away. The herd of ponies grazed in the valley below, moonlight shining on their backs. Her eyes searched the herd. Then she saw him—the pony with the halter. He'd been tamed once. Would he remember?

Here goes nothing, she thought as she walked toward them. The ponies raised their heads and looked at her curiously. They were alert and ready to take off. If they did, they'd be gone for good.

May thought of Stevie Lake, one of the best riders at Pine Hollow Stables. When Stevie wanted to calm a horse, she'd tell it a knock-knock joke.

It can't hurt, May thought.

"Knock knock," May said.

The ponies looked at her with dark, serious eyes.

"Wilfred," she said.

The lead pony, the one that was wearing a halter, stared at her curiously.

"Will fried eggs be okay for breakfast?" May said. As soon as she said it, she knew it was probably one of the worst knock-knock jokes ever told.

The pony shook his head. May had the feeling he was asking if she couldn't do better than that.

"Hey, it was all I could think of," she said.

The pony switched his tail.

"So you tell one," she said. She put her

hands in her pockets and took a step forward.

"Come on," she said in a soft voice.

The pony sighed.

"You wouldn't believe this," May said, taking another slow step, "but there are times I have trouble thinking of knock-knock jokes myself."

The pony nickered. Very gently May touched his neck. He felt like Macaroni—with the same soft pony coat.

"I bet you know a million jokes," she said, looking for his favorite spot. All ponies have a favorite spot.

May moved her hand to a place behind his ears and scratched it gently. The pony looked at her with his big dark eyes as if to say, *How did you know?*

May ran her hand down his neck to his back. This was the scary part. If the pony didn't want to be ridden, he would take off. He turned and looked at her. May could tell he remembered being ridden.

"We're going to have a good time," she said. "We'll have a great ride." She unfastened her belt and slipped it through

the halter rings to make a temporary rein. The pony looked at her curiously.

"I'm going to mount you now," she said, running her hand along his back. She took a deep breath and climbed onto the pony's back. The pony shivered, every muscle alert, ready to run.

"We've got to go back to the farmhouse," May said, looking out over the moor. "But where is it?" When she'd come out here with Dottie and Ellie, she'd been so busy being brave that she hadn't looked where she was going. Now she didn't know how to get back.

"Home," she said. "Wherever that is."

The pony stood there, waiting for her to give him a signal. She sat there wondering what to do. There was a rustling in the heather. What is that? thought May. But she stopped wondering, because suddenly the pony seemed to know which way to go. He nickered and set off over a low hill. He trotted over the hill and down into a bog. He picked his way through the muck and struggled onto dry ground.

With each step he seemed to go faster.

May clutched his mane. Something brushed her face. The moonlight was shattered like broken glass. Dark birds rose past her head, up into the moonlit air.

"Just birds," she said to the pony with a wobble in her voice. "I bet they were as scared as we were." Her heart was pounding so hard that her chest hurt.

The pony stopped suddenly and stood still as if the birds had confused him.

"Keep going," May said, trying to keep her voice casual.

The pony shook his head as if he'd lost the way.

"You can do it," May said.

May saw the heather tremble. It must be the wind, she thought. The pony nodded and headed off again.

May's hair blew back, lifted by the wind. Tears streamed out of her eyes. A rock loomed ahead. The pony jumped the rock. May thought of Max Regnery. If he could see her jumping on the moor in the moonlight, he'd be furious. May knew it was dangerous, but she also knew Ellie was counting on her and the wild pony.

The pony was running downhill. He stumbled and lurched. With no saddle or stirrups, May couldn't hold on. She started to fall. Suddenly the pony slowed. It was as if he knew that May would fall if he kept cantering. May grabbed his mane and pulled herself back into position.

"Okay, boy," she said. "Let's go."

The pony galloped along a creekbed and up a hill.

May looked down and saw the farmhouse shining in the moonlight.

"We made it," she said to the pony. She shook the makeshift rein, and he trotted downhill and through the farmhouse gate.

"Mom!" May shouted. "Dad!"

A light went on. Her mother's head appeared at a window.

"Ellie's hurt," May said. "We've got to get her right away."

A second later Mrs. Grover ran out of the farmhouse. "What happened?" she asked. "What's going on?"

"We went for a walk on the moor," May said.

"At this hour?" Mrs. Grover said. "Without telling us?"

Mr. Grover ran out of the house.

"What's that?" he said, looking at May's pony.

"A wild pony," May said. "He brought me home."

Mr. Grover noticed the belt that May had been using for a rein. "You did a great job, May," he said. "But now you need to ride Cheddar." He held the pony's halter while May slid off his back. Then Mr. Grover led the wild pony into the paddock.

May flew into the barn. Cheddar, who had missed all the excitement, yawned. "This is the biggest job you'll ever have to do," she said to him. "I'm counting on you."

She saddled Cheddar and led him out of the barn. Mr. Grover had saddled Spock, and now he was saddling a pony for Ellie to ride.

Mrs. Grover ran out of the house with a flashlight. She handed it to Mr. Grover.

"The moon has gone behind a cloud,"

she said worriedly. "How are you going to find her?"

"We'll find a way," May said.

But when May and Mr. Grover had ridden out the farm gate and were on the road up to the moor, May turned to him and said, "Finding your way around the moor in the dark is tough. I'm not sure I can find Dottie and Ellie."

"You'll do it," Mr. Grover said.

They walked Spock, Cheddar, and the pony to the top of the hill. When they got there, the moor was covered with white, wispy mist.

May pressed her knees into Cheddar's sides. "Do your best," she said. Reluctantly Cheddar stepped into the cold mist.

"Dad," May said.

"I'm here," her father said.

But she couldn't see him.

"I'll follow the sound of Cheddar's hoofbeats. You lead," Mr. Grover said.

May leaned low over Cheddar's neck and said, "They're near a giant's toothpick."

Cheddar shook his head. He didn't like walking in the mist. He wanted to go home.

"It's important," May said to the pony. "Really, really, really."

Something jolted Cheddar from behind. It was almost as if someone had given him a kick in the rump. Cheddar looked over his shoulder. May looked over her shoulder. But there was no one there. Cheddar took a quick step forward, and then he began to trot.

Mist blew around May's face. It wet her hair. Her windbreaker streamed with water. May thought of Ellie lying on the wet ground. They had to get there fast.

"Go," she said to Cheddar.

The pony went faster.

They seemed to trot forever. And then they trotted more. May was beginning to give up when she heard a faint cry.

"Dad," she called over her shoulder. "I hear them."

"Lead on, May," he said. "You're doing a great job."

"Help!" came a voice.

"We'd better get off our horses and go

the rest of the way on foot," Mr. Grover said.

May slid off Cheddar. The ground beneath her feet was like a sponge. She couldn't believe that Cheddar had been able to trot on it. "Good work," she said to him. "You are a champ."

Carefully May and her father walked forward.

Suddenly there was a gust of wind. The fog rose. Ellie was lying in the grass, her face dead white. Mr. Grover ran the last few steps and knelt next to Ellie. He gently felt her ankle. Ellie moaned again. "It's broken," he said. He looked up at May. "It's a good thing we got here so fast."

He helped Ellie onto the pony. Then he gave Dottie a leg up so that she could ride double, behind May. Slowly they walked back to the farmhouse, unable to go quickly because Ellie was in so much pain.

May wanted to help Ellie think about something besides her broken ankle, so she said, "You know, you may be right about piskies."

"Unh," Ellie said. "What?"

"Someone led the wild pony to the farmhouse. It could have been piskies," May said.

"Give me a break," said Dottie.

"Cheddar didn't want to go onto the moor, but then something made him go anyway," May said.

"Your imagination," said Dottie.

"Piskies aren't real," Mr. Grover said gently. "They're imaginary."

May sighed. Her father was right, of course. There was no such thing as piskies.

When they came to the top of the road, the farmhouse looked bright and inviting. It seemed as if every window was lighted. When they got to the courtyard, Mrs. Grover was waiting with a blanket to wrap around Ellie.

"There's hot chocolate for you girls on the stove," Mrs. Grover said to May and Dottie. "We're taking Ellie to the emergency room. They're waiting for us."

Wrapped in the blanket, Ellie looked pale and scared.

"She's going to be okay, right?" May said to Mr. Grover.

"Thanks to you," he said.

They watched the car drive away.

"Hot chocolate, here I come," said Dottie.

"We have to take care of Spock and the ponies," May said.

Dottie groaned.

"Dottie!" May said. "They brought us home."

"I guess," Dottie grumbled. But as they walked toward the barn, Dottie said, "You know, May, you were okay out there, like brave or something." She reached over and punched May's arm.

"Ouch!" May said, pretending that it hurt. But inside, she felt happy and warm. She knew this might be as close to a compliment as Dottie would ever come.

They had a lot of work to do. Not only did they have to untack the horse and the ponies and give them hay, but they also had to get them settled for the night. May noticed that Dottie had her own way of dealing with ponies. She talked to them

as if they were teenage boys. "Stop act-
ing like a dork," she said to the pony Ellie
had ridden.

Finally they were finished.

"The hot chocolate is now cold chocolate," Dottie said gloomily.

"That's what stoves are for," May said.
"I'm going to say good-night to the wild
pony."

The pony was in the paddock, sniffing
at the fence posts. May went into the
barn and looked for the tastiest, crunchi-
est hay she could find. Finally she found a
bunch that was filled with dried flowers.
She lifted the hay in her arms and carried
it out to the paddock and put it in the
feed trough. The pony was hungry. He
trotted over and started eating it right
away.

This is a pony who knows his way
around paddocks, May thought. She
wondered if he had run away from a
farm like this. Somewhere there was
probably someone who really missed
him. When the pony raised his head,
May reached out and stroked his soft

nose. Then she put her arms around him. "You are the greatest," she said softly.

May leaned against the fence and thought about her wild ride on the moor. She remembered the way the heather had rustled at the pony's feet every time he seemed to be wondering which way to go. It would be wonderful to think that piskies really did exist and that they had helped guide her and the pony home. But she knew they were only a legend. What had been real was how bravely the wild pony had carried her across the dark, windy moor back to the farmhouse and her parents. Suddenly May missed her own house, and her bedroom with its pony posters, and most of all her two best friends and dear, sweet Macaroni. She wished she could take the wild pony home with her so that she'd never have to say good-bye.

The wild pony sighed.

"I know how you feel," May said. "You miss your owner. Tomorrow we'll find her and you'll be safe at home again."

8 The Wild Pony Goes Home

When May woke the next morning, she realized that today was not an ordinary day. Today was the day she was going to reunite the wild pony with his owner. She got dressed as fast as she could and raced downstairs.

Ellie was sitting at the kitchen table with one foot up on a chair. On her foot was a cast. Leaning against the wall was a pair of crutches.

"Wow," May said. "Are you okay?"

"She is not okay," Mrs. Grover said. "She's in big trouble." She looked sternly at May. "I'd like to hear your version of what happened last night."

May noticed that Ellie and Dottie looked nervous.

"We went for a walk on the moor," May said. "No big deal."

"No big deal!" Mrs. Grover said. "I should think it *was* a big deal."

Ellie and Dottie looked at May pleadingly.

"It was a gorgeous moonlit night," May said. "You're always telling us we should get the most out of Cornwall. Well, we did."

"You were being totally irresponsible," said Mrs. Grover.

"The moon was full. The stars were out. It was totally safe," May said.

"I suppose that's why your sister broke her ankle," said Mrs. Grover tartly.

"Sorry, Mom," May said. "I won't ever, ever do it again." That's for sure, May thought. No way would she ever again go running around the moor on a moonlit night.

May got herself a bowl of cereal and a glass of milk and dug in. She was starving. She finished as fast as she could, washed the bowl and glass, and put them in the dish rack. Then she rushed out to the paddock to see the pony.

The paddock was empty! But it can't be empty, she thought. She ran to the gate. It was open. The pony must have pushed the latch up and set himself free.

She raced back into the house. Mr. Grover was pouring himself a cup of coffee.

"The pony's gone," she said breathlessly. "We have to find him."

May and her father walked out to the barn. "It's my fault," May said. "I should have tied him up."

Her father put his arm around her. "It's not your fault."

"We've got to find him," she said.

She went to tack up Cheddar, and Mr. Grover went to tack up Spock.

They met in the courtyard and rode out of the valley to the top of the hill.

Below them, the moor was pink and green and fuzzy with flowers. Butterflies hovered over the blossoms. May could see the sparkle of a half-hidden stream.

They rode and rode, but the ponies were nowhere.

"He's out here somewhere," May said.

As they cantered down the trail, May scanned the moor. Somehow she knew she could find the pony.

They rounded a hill—and there they were. The wild ponies were grazing near the bog where Ellie had broken her ankle.

"Let's go," May said to Mr. Grover.

"Hold on, May," he said.

She turned to look at her father. He had a wistful look.

"He needs us," May said.

"Are you sure?" Mr. Grover said. "He looks pretty happy to me."

For a second May felt like pressing her knees against Cheddar's side to get him to trot forward, but then she looked again. The wild pony raised his head, his mouth full of grass, and chewed contentedly. He stood there for a second, swallowing it, and then he tossed his head and set off at a gallop, the other ponies running after him.

"They're getting away," May said.

The pony ran to a hilltop. He stopped, looking over the moor, ready to run again.

"In a second he'll be gone," May said. She thought about how the pony needed a young rider to love him.

The pony galloped off again with the other ponies behind him. Where are they going? May wondered. Anywhere they want, she guessed. Suddenly she felt sad. She realized that she would never talk to the pony again, never pat him, never feel his soft coat. She didn't need to find him a perfect home. He already had one.

"I guess we'd better go back," she said.

"Not so fast." Mr. Grover turned to her. "He needs you."

"Me?" said May. "I don't think so."

"He needs you to set him free," Mr. Grover said. "That halter is dangerous for him. It can get caught on things. It has to be taken off, and you're the one to do it."

May took a deep breath. This was not what she had planned.

They rode as close to the ponies as they could without scaring them, and then May got off Cheddar and handed the reins to her father.

May walked slowly forward. She felt terrible. Last night they had been getting to know each other, and now they were saying good-bye.

"Knock knock," she said.

The pony lifted his head.

"It's me, with the terrible sense of humor," she said.

The pony stared at her with his big brown eyes.

He came over to her and put his nose in her hair. She reached for the buckle of his halter. The buckle was gummy. It stuck.

"So where's that knock-knock joke you were going to tell me?" she said as she worked at the buckle. The pony shook his head. "You're embarrassed because it's so bad," she said. "There's no shame in a bad knock-knock joke. I tell them all the time."

The pony snorted. The buckle came open. Gently May slid the halter down over his nose.

"See you," she said. "Next full moon, think of me."

The pony pawed and nodded as if that was what he'd been waiting for. He turned and galloped up the hill, with the other ponies following him. The last thing May saw was his tail streaming in the wind.

9 The Girls Take a Gander at Alexander!

"I don't believe it," Jasmine said.

She and Corey had stopped off in the Takamuras' barn to say good-night to Corey's pony, Sam. Once again, Alexander was missing.

"It happens every night," Corey said. "The only problem is that it's impossible."

Jasmine nodded. The door of Samurai's stall was always latched. There was no way Alexander could have gotten out.

"Let's go check May's barn," Jasmine said.

They walked down the Pony Trail to May's barn.

When they got inside, Will was leaning over the door of Macaroni's stall. "Take a gander," he said.

"What?" asked Jasmine.

"I think he means we should look," Corey said.

Jasmine and Corey peered inside the stall. There was Alexander, happily snoozing at Macaroni's side.

"Weird," said Corey and Jasmine together.

"Fantastical," said Will with a grin.

10 Home at Last

On the airplane on the way home, May sat next to her father. After the movie was over, she said, "Can I ask you something?"

Mr. Grover nodded.

"I keep thinking about the wild pony," May said.

Mr. Grover nodded. "Me too."

"Would it be okay if I gave him a name?" May said.

"You set him free," Mr. Grover said. "So you can give him a name."

"I think of him as Swifty," May said.

"Excellent name," Mr. Grover said with a grin.

"He's better off being free," May said.

"He wouldn't be happy otherwise," Mr. Grover said.

May swallowed. She had something hard to ask. "If Swifty wants to be free, do all ponies want to be free?"

Mr. Grover thought about it and said, "Ponies like being trained. They love learning. They love their owners. But I think there's a part of them that wants to run free."

May crossed her arms and clutched her elbows because she hadn't gotten to the really hard question yet. "Do you think Macaroni wants to run free?"

"Macaroni loves you. And he loves the barn. And he loves Sam and Outlaw. But maybe there's a part of him that wants to run free," Mr. Grover said. He grinned again. "Maybe there's a part of you that wants to run free, too, with no school, and no homework, and no chores."

"Totally," May said.

"Maybe that's why you love each other so much," Mr. Grover said. "It's because you understand each other."

After that, May felt a lot better. The

flight attendant came around with orange juice and a snack. May polished them off and snuggled down for a nap. She didn't wake up until it was time for dinner, which was chicken and peas. The chicken was tasty. The peas needed work.

The next day May woke up in her own bed. The Grovers had gotten home so late the night before that she hadn't had a chance to see Corey and Jasmine. She hadn't even gotten to see Macaroni. She jumped out of bed, got dressed, and ran out to the barn.

Macaroni was half asleep. He jumped when she entered the stall.

"Macaroonie!" May said as she put her arms around him. Mac nuzzled her hair and then her ear, and then he moved his head back to get a good look, as if he wanted to make sure it was really her.

"I missed you so much," May said to him. Macaroni nodded. May could tell it had seemed like a long time for him, too.

"I met a pony called Cheddar," she said. "He's great, but not half as great as you." Macaroni sighed as if this was a big load off his mind.

Then it was time to see Corey and Jasmine.

May headed for Corey's house and knocked on the back door.

No one answered. May knocked again.

Doc Tock, Corey's mother, appeared in a white nightgown. She was a vet, so she was always expecting an emergency. "What's wrong?" she said.

"Nothing," May said. "I'm home."

"Oh," Doc Tock said. She yawned and looked at her watch. "Do you know what time it is?"

"No," May said.

"Six-fifteen," Doc Tock said. She grinned. "It's great to have you home, May. I'll get Corey."

A few minutes later Corey came scrambling down the stairs. "May!" They gave each other a big hug.

"Did I miss you!" Corey said.

"Me too," May said.

"We've got to get Jasmine," said Corey.

85

"But we don't want to wake her baby sister," said May.

"I have an idea," said Corey.

They walked to Jasmine's backyard. Corey picked up a pebble and tossed it at Jasmine's window. It pinged softly. A second later Jasmine appeared at the window. "May!" she whispered. "I'll be right down."

A minute later she came scrambling out the back door. She hugged May, and then Corey joined in. They stood there in a big Pony Tail hug.

"Cornwall was great," May said, "but I missed you guys."

"We missed you," Jasmine said.

"It seemed like forever," Corey said.

"Mac thought so, too," May said. "Let's go give him the best grooming ever."

"Totally," said Corey.

Fifteen minutes later Macaroni's coat was gleaming, his mane was fluffy, and his hooves had been polished.

The Pony Tails flopped down on the straw in the empty stall next to his. May told Corey and Jasmine about Swifty.

"When I took his halter off, he looked at me like he was saying thank you. And then he was gone." May sighed. "I'll always miss him."

"You did the right thing," Corey said.

"His home is on the moor," Jasmine said.

"I guess," May said, but she still felt a little sad.

"You know what?" Jasmine said. "You can tell me what Swifty looks like and I'll draw a picture of him and you can hang it on your refrigerator. That way you won't miss him so much."

"That would definitely help," May said.

The three of them lay back in silence, happy to be together again.

"So what was Wilfred like?" May asked.

"He was a bit of all right," Corey said.

May smiled. "I can see you've been learning English English."

"Rather," Jasmine said. The three of them giggled.

"His mother makes a great trifle," said Jasmine.

"I know what a trifle is," May said proudly. "It's a custardy dessert."

"Mrs. Neill's trifles are nothing to trifle with," said Corey.

"Oooo," May said, "I missed those terrible Pony Tail jokes."

"One strange thing happened," Jasmine said. "Every night Alexander got out of Corey's barn and went to visit Macaroni."

"So?" May said.

"Both barn doors were closed. There was no way he could get from one barn to another," Jasmine explained.

"Hmmm, this sounds like a case of piskies," May said.

"You mean those bad little invisible things?" asked Corey.

"Piskies aren't bad. They're mischievous," May said. "Not that I believe in them or anything."

"Of course not," said Corey.

"But if there were piskies, that's just the kind of thing they'd do. They'd take Alexander to Macaroni's stall to keep him company," May said. And they'd lead a wild pony and his rider through a moor to get help for someone who was hurt, she thought.

"How would piskies get here?" Jasmine said. "Cornwall is about a million miles away."

May grinned. "Maybe they came in Wilfred's suitcase. Piskies need vacations, too."

"Or maybe it was Will," Corey said with a laugh. "He may be quiet, but he has a great sense of humor."

"Umm," said Jasmine, thinking about it.

"We'll never know," said May happily. "It's a . . ."

The three Pony Tails looked at each other and said, "mystery!"

And then, since they had said the same thing at the same time, they followed an old Pony Tail custom. They gave each other high fives and said, "Jake!"

MAY'S TIPS
ON WILD PONIES

When my family and I went to England, I learned a lot. I already knew what a nuisance my sisters could be, and I already knew how wonderful ponies could be, but I learned even more about both of those things.

Those wild ponies were the first wild ponies I'd ever seen. I'll never forget them, and if you ever see wild ponies, you won't forget them, either.

There aren't very many wild ponies left in the world. Of course, at one time all ponies were wild. It wasn't until people learned to train them and ride them that there was anything but wild ponies. That's called domesticating. Today most horses and ponies are domesticated. In fact, they've never lived in the wild at all, and they probably couldn't survive without people any more than your pet dog or cat could survive if you weren't there to open the cans of food for them.

But there are still some wild ponies around, and I've got to tell you, I don't think I've ever seen anything quite as beautiful as that herd of ponies running free on the moor in England.

In England, two different kinds of ponies can be found in the wild. There are Dartmoor ponies and Exmoor ponies. They're similar and are probably related, but they live in different areas and do have differences. They're about the same size, but the Dartmoor has a thicker neck and a smaller head. The Exmoor's legs are a little shorter than the Dartmoor's and its body is a little stockier. They're both great riding ponies—as my trip across the moor showed me—and lots of children have learned a lot about riding with trained Dartmoor and Exmoor ponies.

There are some other wild ponies in Europe, too. The best known of these are the Camargue ponies. They live in the marshes of southern France. They're tough and strong. All of them are gray—they look almost white. Sometimes people round them up and train them, the same way cowboys used to round up mustangs in the American West and train them to herd cattle.

All the wild horses we know about in the United States actually came from Europe. When people came to conquer North and South America or to settle here, they brought horses with them. Sometimes those horses ran away, and that's how we got wild ponies over here. Out in the American West, there are herds of wild ponies that live on land the government owns. They are protected by the U.S. Bureau of Land Management. When the herds get too large, the government rounds up some of the ponies, and people can adopt them. Before they're allowed to adopt, the people have to prove that they can take care of the ponies, and if they don't do a good job, the Bureau of Land Management takes the ponies back!

We have some wild ponies closer to my town of Willow Creek, too, and I bet you've heard about them. They live on Assateague Island, off the coast of my home state of Virginia. A lot of people have ideas about how the ponies got there in the first place. Nobody knows for sure, of course, but my favorite theory is that they came off a ship that was wrecked in a storm. It must have been an awful storm if the ponies survived and there weren't enough people who survived to round up the ponies, but it shows you what great swimmers those ponies are. Anyway, the ponies are there, and they live in a sanctuary where they can run free. Once a year people round up a herd and make them swim across a channel to a nearby island called Chincoteague, where some of them are auctioned off to buyers, who train them and ride them.

Does this sound familiar to you? If it does, you've probably read one of my favorite books. It's called *Misty of Chincoteague,* and it's by Marguerite Henry. That's a story about the pony-penning, which is what they call the auctioning of the ponies. I must have read that book a zillion times, and each time I read it I like it more. Reading about ponies isn't the same as riding them, but it's the next-best thing.

Today most of the ponies and horses in the world belong to people. They are raised by people, trained by people, and ridden by people. That's been good for the horses and ponies, and it's been good for the people, too. It's been especially good for me and my friends because we're pony-crazy. It scares me to think of Macaroni living out in the wild without me to take care of him, and I'm pretty sure it would scare Macaroni, too. But I've got to tell you, seeing the herd of wild ponies made me understand something about ponies that I'd never understood before. No matter how much we love and take care of our ponies, no matter how much they need us and rely on us, they all have ancestors who lived in the wild.

Now when I look at Macaroni, Outlaw, and Samurai, I know there's a part of their hearts that is, and always will be, wild. I love that part of Macaroni just as much as I love the part that needs me.

About the Author

Bonnie Bryant was born and raised in New York City, and she still lives there today. She spends her summers in a house on a lake in Massachusetts.

Ms. Bryant began writing about girls and horses when she started The Saddle Club series in 1987. So far there are more than fifty books in that series. Much as she likes telling the stories about Stevie, Carole, and Lisa, she decided that the younger riders at Pine Hollow, especially May Grover, have stories of their own that need telling. That's how Pony Tails was born.

Ms. Bryant rides horses when she has time away from her computer, but she doesn't have a horse of her own. She likes to ride different horses and enjoys a variety of riding experiences. She says she thinks most of her readers are much better riders than she is!

*Look for Bonnie Bryant's next exciting
Pony Tails adventure
in bookstores in June 1997*

COREY'S SECRET FRIEND
Pony Tails #12

Someone is doing nice things for Corey.
She thinks it's one of her best friends,
Jasmine or May. Then she learns it's not!
Who is Corey's secret friend? One
thing's for sure—this person is doing
nice things for Corey just when she
needs them most. Her mom has started
dating, and Corey isn't sure how she
feels about the man or his daughter,
Alice, who's Corey's age. Is Alice about
to become part of Corey's family?

Win riding lessons and a saddle!

Sweepstakes sponsored by

STATE LINE TACK®
The Discount Tack Store

Hurry— enter to win!

Return completed entry to:
Bantam Doubleday Dell, Attn: Free Riding Lessons, 1540 Broadway, 20th floor, New York, NY 10036

Name _____

Address _____

City _____ State _____ Zip _____

Date of Birth _____ / _____ / _____
                              Month   Day   Year

HORSE CRAZY SWEEPSTAKES OFFICIAL RULES

I. ELIGIBILITY

No purchase necessary. Enter by completing and returning the Official Entry Form. All entries must be received by Bantam Doubleday Dell postmarked no later than July 15, 1997. No mechanically reproduced entries allowed. By entering the sweepstakes, each entrant agrees to be bound by these rules and the decision of the judges which shall be final and binding. Limit one entry per person.

The sweepstakes is open to children between the ages of 4 and 15 years of age (as of July 15, 1997), who are residents of the United States and Canada, excluding the Province of Quebec. The winner, if Canadian, will be required to answer correctly a time-limited arithmetic skill question in order to receive the prize. Employees of Bantam Doubleday Dell Publishing Group, Inc., and its subsidiaries and affiliates and their immediate family members are not eligible. Void where prohibited or restricted by law. Grand Prize will be awarded in the name of a parent or legal guardian.

II. PRIZE

The prize is as follows:

One Grand Prize: Approximate Retail Value - $1,000 consists of: $500 worth of riding lessons at the stable of your choice and one of the following three saddles: Collegiate Prep All-Purpose-Child's (retail: $435), Collegiate Alumnus All-Purpose-Adult (retail: $475), SLT Cambridge Prix D'Ecole-Adult (retail: $649).

III. WINNER

Winner will be chosen in a random drawing on or about August 15, 1997, from among all completed entry forms. Winner will be notified by mail. Odds of winning depend on the number of entries received. No substitution or transfer of the prize is allowed. All entries become the property of BDD and will not be returned. Taxes, if any, are the sole responsibility of the winner. BDD RESERVES THE RIGHT TO SUBSTITUTE A PRIZE OF EQUAL VALUE IF PRIZE, AS STATED ABOVE, BECOMES UNAVAILABLE. Winner and their legal guardian will be required to execute and return, within 14 days of notification, affidavit of eligibility and release. A non-compliance within that time period or the return of any prize notification as undeliverable will result in disqualification and the selection of an alternate winner. In the event of any other non-compliance with rules and conditions, prize may be awarded to an alternate winner. For a list of winners (available after August 15, 1997), send a self-addressed, stamped envelope entirely separate from your entry to: Bantam Doubleday Dell, Attn: Riding Winners, 1540 Broadway, 20th floor, New York, NY, 10036. Return completed entry to: Bantam Doubleday Dell, Attn: Free Riding Lessons, 1540 Broadway, 20th floor, New York, NY 10036.

BFYR 137